Tickles Tale

Written by Stephen Cosgrove
Illustrated by Robin James

A Serendipity™ *Book*

PSS!
PRICE STERN SLOAN

The Serendipity™ series was created by Stephen Cosgrove and Robin James

Copyright © 1989, 2001 by Price Stern Sloan. All rights reserved.
Published by Price Stern Sloan, a division of
Penguin Putnam Books for Young Readers, New York.

Printed in Hong Kong. Published simultaneously in Canada. No part of this publication may be
reproduced, stored in any retrieval system, or transmitted, in any form or by any means, electronic,
mechanical, photocopying, recording, or otherwise, without the prior written permission of the publisher

Library of Congress Catalog Card Number: 89-60565

ISBN 0-8431-7664-4

2001 Revised Edition

PSS! is a registered trademark of Penguin Putnam Inc.
Serendipity and the pink dragon are trademarks of Penguin Putnam Inc.

Dedicated to my daughter, Julie,
and all her wonderful cats.
– Stephen

ar beyond the horizon, in the middle of the Crystal Sea is a magical island that is known as Serendipity. All in all, on the island of Serendipity, there was very little of what you would call magic beyond, of course, your imagination.

Even so, on Crystal Mountain, near the stilled waters of the Lake of Mirrors, stood a small stone castle where odd, magical things truly happened. Here, lightning flashed and rainbows arched above the walls of the castle on perfectly clear days.

This was the castle of the wistful Wizard Wink, master of illusion and magic.

Wizard Wink was a kind and gentle wizard who actually read about magic more than he whizzed his wizardry. He would sit for hours bathed in the golden light that streamed like ribbons through windows opened wide, reading books about this and that.

Around him on dusty shelves and a rickety table were powders and potions stored in vials and vases. There was twiddle dust, dream steam, flim flummery and other such puffery much needed and used daily by the wizard in his trade.

Although he knew other wizards, Wink didn't have many friends that slept over or even dropped by for tea, for they were just as reclusive as he.

What he had instead and who was still a friend indeed, was a bright white cat called Tickles. He was called Tickles because he loved to tickle his own pink nose with his short, fluffy tail as he ran around and around trying to touch one to the other.

Tickles would tickle and turn, turn and tickle, until the tickles turned into sniggles and the sniggles into giggles and the giggles became gales of laughter. Well, as much as a cat could laugh, which was more like a muffled meow.

Tickles had the full run of the castle and he would prowl about, as cats were wont to do. Often he would hunt hidden magical mice that never seemed to be found.

But, mostly he would spend his days curled in a warm ray of sunshine on a nice wide shelf. From his lofty perch he would watch with a lazy eye as Wizard Wink read from his book of magic and whisked and whipped his potent potions.

Now the wizard didn't have many rules and the rules he had were simple and brief: Sip your milk; don't slurp; and never, ever mess with the magic. That was all! There were no others.

Content with the fact that Tickles understood the rules, the wizard set out one day for the village and left the cat all alone.

"Take care, my little, fuzzy friend,"said he as he put on his wizard's cap and traveling coat, "for I won't be long." With that he was out the castle door as Tickles' tail whipped sassily about. "Meow!"

The one thing about cats that make them almost magical and slightly mysterious is their curiosity and Tickles had tons.

"Harrumm," he thought as he stretched and arched his back, "I'm very curious, is there any milk in my dish?" With that he pussyfooted across the wizard's table and jumped to the floor below.

He padded about the castle, looking for his saucer but look though he may, no dainty dish could be found.

"Harrumm," purred Tickle as he rubbed his tickly tail around a ladder's rail, "curiously, when there is no milk there are always mice. Beyond milk, mice are nice, very nice indeed."

Off he ran to look about for any mighty mouse or many mice that might be skittering about that would make a wonderful meal.

Tickles looked here, Tickles looked there, but nowhere could he find some mice or for that matter even one single mouse. He looked in the gnawed hole in the castle wall; usually there was one or two in there but not today. He looked in the un-tripped trap in the dusty hall, but it was empty too.

He looked and looked but look though he may, Tickles found nothing, nothing at all. And he was most hungry indeed.

It was at this time that curiosity, tainted with a bit of hunger, got the best of Tickles, the wizard's cat. He happened to find himself on the rickety table looking about for something to eat. With his tail idly twitching from side to side, he sat there in a pool of light, on the wizard's book of magic delight.

Tickles looked around and a round and then he looked down. It was then that he saw the most curious words indeed:

"If hungry you are, if starvation you fear
say these words and food will appear.
'Hocus pocus lavender locust
brighten my eyes, bring dinner into focus.'"

Below these words was this ominous warning:

"Don't use this magic more times than two,
though hungry indeed or curious are you!"

Curiosity will always get the cat and Tickles was no exception. Quickly he meowed the words out loud while thinking of gallons and gallons of milk.

At first, nothing happened, but then the skies turned purple, then crickled and cracked as lightning flashed and thunder crashed.

When all became light again, Tickle looked about for his magical meal but there was nothing there; no saucer, no milk. The floor was bare.

Beyond his sight, through the window bright, the stilled waters of the Lake of Mirrors turned from water to rich lappable cream but Tickles didn't see.

"Harrumm," he purred, "maybe I should try it again."

With his eyes scrunched tight, he meowed the words loudly until they echoed all through the castle. This time, as he chanted, he thought and thought of the largest plumpest mouse he might. Once again, the skies flashed with lightning and crashed with thunderous roars. But still it appeared that nothing happened. Nothing happened at all.

Nothing happened, that is, save for just out of Tickles' sight, a mouse the size of a house rushed from the castle and galloped into the mountains beyond.

Now the warning was still on the page, *"Never use this magic more times than two, though hungry indeed and curious are you."* As we all know cats rarely read something more than once and Tickles' curiosity was teased by the hunger in his belly.

Without regard to the consequence, he chanted the magical words once again,
"Hocus pocus lavender locust
brighten my eyes bring dinner into focus,"

But this time, the third time, there was no thunder, no lightning. This time, the third time, there was only a puff of purple dust and a special spark that settled about the cat. Tickles didn't have time for worry or wonder at this odd event, for out the window he spied the Wizard Wink wandering up the path and back to the castle keep.

Tickles looked about to make sure that all was in order, and then he leaped to the shelf where he always slept. There, he plopped himself down and with one eye open, he pretended to be asleep. Just in time, it would seem, as the wizard waltzed in the door carrying a polished pine pitcher, nothing more.

The wizard shook his head curiously as he scratched his long, white beard. "Hmm," said he, "all of this is a bit odd. The Lake of Mirrors has turned into cream and I was passed on the road by a mouse the size of a house. Whose magic could this be?"

The Wizard Wink looked and looked but nothing seemed to be amiss. The vials and vases were where they should be and the magical book was open just as he had left it.

"Harrumph," grumbled he as he shook his head, "all this must have been an old wizard's imagination."

With one eye cracked open and the other asleep, Tickles watched and waited but nothing happened, nothing happened at all.

The wizard busily bustled about as he whistled a tune and poured some milk from the pitcher into a dainty dish. Once filled, he put it on the floor.

"There, my Tickles,"he said as he stroked the cat. "I knew you must be hungry, so I slipped into the village while you slept and bought you a fresh pitcher of milk." Without further ado, the wizard went back to work and Tickles lapped at his dinner, delighted with his deception. Ah, yes, he was very relieved that that he hadn't been caught.

THE WIZARD HAD HIS RULES

AND TICKLES BROKE THEM, TRUE.

WHEN WRONG YOU'LL ALWAYS GET CAUGHT

NOT BY HIM, OR THEM, BUT . . . YOU!

Although . . .

. . .This curious cat did break the rules
He did what was very wrong
And though he never did get caught,
Tickles' tail is now three feet long.

Serendipity™ Books

Created by
Stephen Cosgrove and Robin James

Enjoy all the delightful books in the Serendipity™ Series:

Available wherever books are sold.

PSS!
PRICE STERN SLOAN